HERE COMES
LOLO

To Busisiwe from Niki,
with deep admiration

Text and illustrations copyright © Niki Daly 2019
First published in Great Britain in 2019 by
Otter-Barry Books, Little Orchard, Burley Gate,
Herefordshire, HR1 3QS
www.otterbarrybooks.com

A catalogue record for this book is available from the British Library

ISBN 978-1-910959-77-0

Illustrated with digital art

Set in Maiandra GD

Printed in Great Britain

9 8 7 6 5 4 3 2 1

HERE COMES
LOLO

Written and illustrated by Niki Daly

Otter-Barry BOOKS

Contents

A Gold Star and a Kiss for Lolo

Friday was always the big day of the Star Awards. So far, Lolo had earned a yellow star for her Maths sums, a red star for her neat writing and a blue star for clean hands. Green stars were for helping Mrs McKensie carry her big bag from her car to the classroom, and gold stars were for reading. Gold stars rocked!

Stars were always awarded just before the school bell rang at the end of the day, when everyone rushed out to meet their mums, dads, grannies or aunts in the playground.

Everyone except Lolo, who lived
close by and could walk home. Lolo
lived with her mama at the back of her
Gogo's dressmaking shop.

Fridays were also great because Lolo got money to buy a treat on her way home. And this Friday was an extra lucky day because Lolo reached the car park just in time to help Mrs McKensie carry her big bag to the classroom. Maybe she'd win a green star... Although a gold star for reading would be better, of course.

Lately, Lolo had made a special effort with her reading – to read with expression, to pause after a comma and to stop at a full stop to catch her breath. Brendan, who the children called "Greedy Eyes" because he devoured so many books, was the best reader.

Lolo helped Mrs McKensie hand out worksheets. Friday's worksheet was all about time – which was going far too slowly for Lolo.

If only she could make all the hands on the clocks spin and stop at Star Awards time!

During music, Lolo couldn't wait for the last line of a new song to end.

Waiting for the Star Awards was
painful.

The final part of the school day was 'free time', so Lolo decided to read. And while she read – first one book, then another and another – she forgot all about time.

By the time she had added the titles to her reading list, Mrs McKensie was ready to announce the star winners.

Shane, Rhapelang and
Corné got yellow stars. Gift,
Aydon, Cleo and Kay-Lee got
red stars. Busi got a green
star. And Dana Rose, who
had managed to wash green
glitter off her fingers during
break, got a blue star.
Then Lolo heard her
name being called!

"Lolo and Brendan," announced Mrs McKensie, looking through the reading lists.

Brendan had read five books and Lolo had read six! She felt like melting with happiness as Mrs McKensie placed a gold star on her forehead.

"*Clang-a-lang!*" went the school bell. Lolo raced through the school gates; she couldn't wait to show Mama and Gogo her gold star.

When she reached Mrs Ismail's spicy doughnut stand, her face was hot from running. Mrs Ismail's little daughter, Sharifa, was pretending to be a shopkeeper. She handed Lolo a spicy doughnut in a paper bag and smiled sweetly.

"Thank you," said Lolo and sped off.

"Mama! Gogo!" she called, bursting through the front door. "Look what I got!"

Gogo looked up from her sewing and Mama peeped around a corner.

"*Molo*, Lolo!" they said. "Hello, how was school?"

"Look!" said Lolo. Mama and Gogo looked while Lolo pointed to her forehead.

"Look at what, Lolo?" asked Gogo.

"My gold star!" said Lolo impatiently.

"What gold star?" asked Mama.

"*This one*," said Lolo, running a finger across her forehead. But all she felt was smooth skin. The gold star had gone!

Lolo burst into tears as she explained how she had received a gold star for reading.

"Where did you have it last?" asked Mama.

"At school," replied Lolo.

"And what did you do after school?" asked Gogo.

In tears, Lolo went over her route from school.

"Well, it's only a paper star," said Mama.

But it wasn't. It was a very special *gold* star.

"Dry your tears. We'll go and look for your gold star," said Gogo.

Gogo helped Lolo retrace her steps round the corner and along the road back to school.

And there, at Mrs Ismail's doughnut stand, they found Lolo's gold star, stuck to the forehead of Mrs Ismail's little girl!

When Mrs Ismail heard Lolo's sad story, she said, "Sharifa darling, that gold star you picked up belongs to Lolo."

But little Sharifa had fallen in love with Lolo's gold star.

And when Mrs Ismail tried to remove it, Sharifa screamed so loudly that people thought something terrible was happening.

Gogo turned to Lolo. "Sharifa's too small to understand what is fair. But you are old enough to be thoughtful. Let her keep your gold star," she said.

Lolo thought for a while. The corners of the gold star had curled up and it looked as if it were about to fall off again. "OK," said Lolo, "Sharifa can keep it."

But inside, she still felt sad. Gold stars were not that easy to win.

Then at bedtime, Gogo brought Lolo something special she had made: a glittery gold star on a hairclip.

"That's for being such a good reader," said Gogo.

Then she kissed Lolo on the forehead and whispered, "And *that's* for being such a kind, thoughtful girl."

Lolo touched her forehead and thought a little more as she drifted off to sleep: gold stars get curly corners and fall off, but kisses last forever!

Lolo's Hat

Lolo fell in love with the hat the moment she saw it. It was floppy with blue and yellow stripes and a big pink flower right in the middle – it was the prettiest hat she had ever seen. She stood looking at it, wishing it was on her head instead of on the stand in a window of Fashion Corner.

"Are you shopping with your eyes, Lolo?" asked Mama.

"Yes, Mama," said Lolo, "I love that hat *so* much!"

"Well, I don't have money for it now. But, maybe, when I get paid at the end of the week I'll buy it for you... if you're good."

"I'll be good, Mama," said Lolo.

The days went by slowly. Every night Lolo hoped she would dream about her new hat. And one night she did! She dreamed she was wearing it when a wind suddenly lifted it off her head and blew it away!

When she told Mama about her terrible dream, Mama said, "Don't worry, Lolo. Tomorrow is Friday and I will be paid a bit more money for some extra work. I will go to Fashion Corner and buy your hat before I come home."

The next day, Lolo couldn't wait for Mama
to come home. While she sat at the kitchen
table watching Gogo make supper, she kept
asking every few minutes: "When will Mama
come home?"

"When will Mama come home?"

"Lolo, you are driving me crazy! Your mama will be home when she's home!" said Gogo.

Well, Lolo didn't know what *that* meant, so she asked again, "But *when* will Mama come home?"

Gogo rolled her eyes, put her hands on her hips and sighed. Lolo knew what *that* meant: Gogo was losing her patience.

So, before that could happen, Lolo went to her room, got out her paints and painted a picture of herself wearing her beautiful new hat.

And just as she finished, she heard the front door open and Mama say, "Molo, Gogo. Where's Lolo?"

Lolo rushed into the kitchen. She could tell something was wrong straight away.

"Lolo," Mama said, "I'm sorry. Your hat was the last one they had, and it was already sold."

Lolo felt as though her tummy had turned upside down and inside out! She burst into tears.

"That is not the only hat in the world, Lolo," said Gogo.

But Lolo was heartbroken. She loved that hat so much. Nothing Gogo and Mama said would change that. It had gone, gone!

That Sunday, Lolo was still sad.

As they walked to church, Gogo said, "I'm
going to say a special prayer for you, Lolo,
so that you will be happy again."

But there was no chance of that happening because, as they entered the church, Lolo saw something that made her tummy turn upside down and inside out once again. There was Thandi Makalima... wearing *her* hat!

"I can't believe it," whispered Mama. "I told Thandi's mother about the hat I was going to buy for Lolo. She must have gone and bought it for her daughter!"

When is was time to pray, Lolo couldn't even close her eyes. All she could think of was – how could her hat end up on someone else's head! *How?*

After church, they couldn't avoid walking home alongside the Makalimas. The wind was blowing and Thandi had to hold on to her hat.

"I hate this hat!" said Thandi. "It's too small and keeps slipping off my head." With that, she took it off and gave it to Lolo. "Here, you can have it," she said.

"But what will your mama say?" asked Lolo.

"I'll tell her the wind blew it away," said Thandi. "She won't mind."

But Mrs Makalima did mind!

Later, when Mama opened the front door and Lolo saw Thandi and her angry mother standing in the wind, she knew exactly what they had come for.

"Lolo," said Mama, "take Thandi to your room. Mrs Makalima and I need to talk."

When they were alone in her room, Lolo asked, "Is your mama very cross?"

"Yes," said Thandi. "She didn't believe the wind blew that silly hat off my head."

"It's a beautiful hat," said Lolo, picking up her painting to show Thandi. "See? That's me wearing it."

"*You* painted this?" gasped Thandi. "It's *beoooootiful!*" And before Lolo could say "thanks", Thandi ran off with Lolo's painting to show her mother.

41

"Look at Lolo's amazing painting," said Thandi.

"That is lovely," said Mrs Makalima, smiling. Mama was also smiling.

"Mrs Makalima has agreed for me to buy Thandi's hat," said Mama.

"Or," said Mrs Makalima, "I will swap it for Lolo's painting. It will look stunning framed and hanging in Thandi's bedroom."

"Cool!" cried Thandi. "I'd love that."

"So, is everyone happy?" asked Gogo.

"I'm happy," said Mama.

"I'm happy," said Mrs Makalima.

"I'm super-happy," said Thandi.

"And how about you, Lolo?" asked Gogo.

Lolo put on the pretty hat that finally belonged to her, and smiled.

Lolo didn't have to say anything!

Lolo and the Lost Ring

Whenever Mama, Gogo and Lolo went for a walk, Mama would look up and say, "I love the clouds against the blue sky." Gogo would look around and say, "I love those trees," or "What a nice dress that woman is wearing." Stuff like that.

Lolo liked looking at the ground where flowers grew and where there are cracks to jump over on pavements.

And that's where she found it: a ring lying in a crack on the pavement!

It wasn't one of those play-play rings you get in surprise packets. It wasn't one of those cheap rings from the market that Mama could afford. This was a real ring that was made of gold and had bright sparkly stones, a big one in the middle and two little ones on each side.

"Look what I've found, Mama!" said Lolo.

Mama took the ring out of Lolo's hand and had a good look.

"This looks like a very special ring," said Mama. Mama slipped it onto one of her fingers.

It fitted perfectly. Gogo leaned over and said, "Finders keepers!"

"Can we keep it?" asked Lolo.

"No," said Mama, "this looks like an engagement ring. We must find the person who lost it and give it back."

"The lady who lost this must be very, very sad to have lost her engagement ring," said Lolo. "Now she won't be able to get married."

"It's not as bad as that," said Mama. "But it's very sad to lose such a precious ring."

When they returned home, Gogo made
tea and they sat down to decide how to find
the owner of the ring.

"We can put an ad in the newspaper,
asking if anyone has lost a ring along the
main road," said Mama.

I can draw a picture of the ring!

Bad idea! The person who calls must tell us what it looks like before we hand it over. Only the *real* owner will know that.

That's true! But I'm sure Lolo will make a beautiful poster.

Lolo was starting to feel quite excited
about making a poster that would help to
find the lady who had lost her ring. She got
out her drawing pad, her felt tips and glitter
glue and began making a poster.

In big letters she wrote RING FOUND and
in smaller figures Mama's telephone number.
Then she made a flower border using all her
brightest colours.

And finally, to make the poster really
special, she added blobs of glitter glue in the
middle of each flower.

"That's what I call a fabulous poster," said Gogo. "Let's go and put it up where you found the ring."

And there, outside the art centre, was a pole just the right size to tie the poster to.

"Now we must wait and see who calls," said Gogo.

Well, no sooner had they got back home when Mama's phone rang.

"Hello, I'm phoning about the ring I lost," said a gruff voice.

"I see," said Mama, "will you please tell me what your ring looks like?"

"It's a big ring," said the man. "Well, not *that* big, but it has a *big* diamond."

Mama could tell that the man was making it all up. So she said, "I'm sorry, but we did not find your ring."

And that was that!

"*Eish!*" said Mama, "there are so many 'chancers' out there."

Gogo said, "It sounds as though he was taking a BIG chance."

During the week, two more chancers called. One said her ring was silver, the other said the ring had a moonstone heart.

Lolo started to feel disappointed. The last time she saw her poster on the pole it looked a little bit torn by the wind. Perhaps they would never find the lady who had lost her ring. How sad.

Then one morning a young woman called and described her lost ring. "It's my engagement ring and it has three diamonds on a gold band."

"That's right," said Mama, "please come and collect your ring."

When Mama shared the good news, Lolo cried, "Yay! Can we have tea and biscuits to celebrate?"

"Yes," said Gogo. "After all those chancers, let's celebrate someone who is honest."

And what a lovely celebration it was!

"I'll never take my ring off again," said Belinda, the young lady. "But I teach art at the art centre on Saturday mornings, and I didn't want my ring to get any paint on it.

It must have fallen out when I took out my car keys."

Belinda told them all about her handsome boyfriend, Sam, who she was going to marry. "And I want you all to come to my wedding," said Belinda.

And that was not all she said!

When she learned that Lolo had made the
beautiful poster, she said, "Lolo, for being
such an honest girl, I'd
like to reward you
by inviting you to
join my art class
every Saturday
morning –
for free!"

Lolo just loved that!

Here's Lolo's beautiful picture of Belinda and Sam's wedding.

See! Mama's looking up at the sky, Gogo's looking around at the pretty dresses. And there's Lolo, looking at the ground that's covered in confetti – glittering like diamonds in the sun.

Lolo and a Dog Called Hope

In Lolo's backyard stood a small shed that Lolo loved to climb onto.

From high up, she could look into
the neighbours' backyards. In the new
neighbour's backyard, Lolo noticed a dog,
tied to a packing case with a bit of rope.

She also noticed that when the old dog barked, a man would come out of the house and shout, "Shut up, Mutt!" It didn't even seem to have a proper name. And if it didn't stop barking, the man would give it a kick.

Its bony body looked like an old brown sack with holes in it. The skin round its neck where the rope was tied looked raw. Lolo didn't like what she saw.

When she told Mama and Gogo about
the poor animal, Mama said, "Lolo, you
shouldn't be spying on neighbours."

"I agree," said Gogo. "It's better to mind
your own business."

But Lolo felt sorry for the old dog with
no name.

When winter came, the dog with no name lay on wet cement. It didn't even have the energy to bark any more. Lolo wondered how anyone could be so cruel as the neighbour who shouted at it, kicked it, and called it "Mutt".

But it was no use talking to Mama or Gogo. Whenever she told them what she saw, they said, "Lolo, it is not our business."

Still, Lolo could not forget about the old dog.

At art class she drew a picture of the
poor animal.

When Belinda asked about her picture,
Lolo told the story of the dog with no name.

"People are not allowed to be cruel to
animals, Lolo," said Belinda.

"But Mama says it is not our business," Lolo explained.

"I understand what your mama means," said Belinda. "But animals can't talk, so we must make sure that they do not suffer."

Lolo looked at her picture and tears came to her eyes.

"Listen, Lolo," said Belinda, "I'll talk to Mama and Gogo about it. There must be something we can do for the poor animal."

And there was.

Belinda explained to Mama that the Animal Rescue Service sends an officer to rescue dogs who are mistreated.

"Rescued dogs are fed and kept safely in kennels until someone who really loves dogs gives them a home," explained Belinda.

But Mama was still worried. "What if the man finds out that we told the Animal Rescue people about his dog? He looks very nasty."

"Don't worry about that. The Animal Rescue team don't tell bad people the names of good people who have reported them."

"Are you sure?" asked Gogo.

"I'm sure," said Belinda. "Don't worry."

So it was decided that Belinda would let the Animal Rescue Service know about the dog with no name.

The following week, a van with *Animal Rescue Service* written on it stopped outside the nasty neighbour's house. A big man in a uniform got out and went up to the neighbour's front door.

"Go and see what's happening around the back, Lolo," whispered Gogo.

Around the back, Lolo could see and hear what was going on.

"See?" said the neighbour, trying to sound nice. "I give my dog water and she has her own place to sleep." The rescue man bent down and felt the dog's bony body.

"This dog has been badly treated and is starving. I'm taking her with me to look after," he said. "And I will also let the police know about the boxes I've seen in your house."

"What do you mean?" growled the man in his nasty voice. "Those boxes are filled with my old clothes."

"Old clothes in new computer boxes?" said the rescue man. "I don't think so!"

From the kitchen, Mama and Gogo saw the rescue man gently place the dog with no name into the back of the van. Soon after they had gone, the police arrived.

Inside the house, they found stolen
computers and arrested the nasty neighbour.

"Well, I'm glad that's the end of that!"
sighed Gogo. But it wasn't quite the end...

Belinda adopted the old dog with no name and called her Hope.

On some Saturdays Belinda takes Hope to the art centre where the children get to see how well she is looking.

And Hope always goes to Lolo first.